A House, A Home

Brooke Goffstein

A House,
A Home

Harper & Row, Publishers

A House, A Home
Copyright © 1989 by Brooke Goffstein
Printed in the U.S.A. All rights reserved.
Typography by Al Cetta
1 2 3 4 5 6 7 8 9 10
First Edition

Library of Congress Cataloging-in-Publication Data
Goffstein, M. B.
    A house, a home / Brooke Goffstein.
        p.   cm.
    "A Charlotte Zolotow book."
    Summary: Presents the anatomy and soul of a house as seen through
a camera's eye.
    ISBN 0-06-022436-3 : $. — ISBN 0-06-022437-1 (lib. bdg.) : $
    [1. Dwellings—Fiction.]   I. Title.
PZ7.G5573Ho 1989   88-37376
[E]—dc19   CIP
                                                                    AC

To David

Thanks always to Al Cetta, Melinda Joseph,
and Al Eiseman and the printers at Eastern Press.

A house has skin

and eyes

and bone,

a head,

a breast,

a heart.

We move around

inside a house,

and look out through its eyes.

What the house sees,

we see.

What it feels,

we feel more gently.

Our backs grow against its steps.

Its porch welcomes sunlight

and offers shade.

Our jokes and songs

rise to its ceilings,

and rest beneath its roof.

We'll lovingly restore
its cracked and peeling paint,

lovingly replace
its broken windowpanes,

repair its frame,

mend its roof,

sweep its porch,

and warm its hearth.

Let the tunes fly!